A GOLDEN BOOK • NEW YORK

DISNEY · PIXAR

Cars

Adapted by Ben Smiley
Illustrated by Jean-Paul Orpiñas and Scott Tilley
Designed by Winnie Ho

Lightning McQueen was a race car! He was *flashy* red and had a **SHINY** lightning bolt on his side.

He even had adoring fans.

But he also had a **BiG** problem. His pit crews kept quitting. You see, Lightning thought he could do everything by himself.

And since all Lightning cared about was winning races, he didn't have any friends . . .

except **Mack**.

Mack the truck drove Lightning to all his races.

One night, Lightning wanted to get to a **really BiG** race really fast. He made Mack drive too long, and the loyal truck got **tired**.

Mack swerved, and Lightning fell out the back of the truck! **Uh-oh!**

Lightning had been sleeping.
But he woke up fast! The race car
was **LOST** and *scared*!

Soon he was
racing toward a
forgotten old
town called
Radiator
Springs.

Sheriff chased Lightning. Lightning was scared, so he drove *faster* ! He knocked into just about everything in the little town.

What a mess!

When the chase was over, Lightning had ruined the town's main street. He was in a heap of **trouble**.

In fact, Sheriff had him towed to jail for all the damage he had done.

Only one car in town was friendly to Lightning—
a rusty tow truck named Mater. Mater didn't know
that Lightning was a famous car. He just wanted to
make a new **friend**.

Soon Lightning was brought to court. He thought he would be set free because he was **a superstar race car**.

He was right—almost. Doc, the town's judge, told Lightning to leave town and never come back. He didn't like race cars.

Then Sally, a blue sports car, arrived. She was a lawyer. Lightning thought Sally was pretty.

But Sally just wanted Lightning to fix the mess he had made.

The townsfolk agreed. They loved their town. So Sally and Doc made a deal: Lightning could leave **AFTER** he fixed the road.

Accused

But Lightning was still in a rush to get to his big race. So he worked too fast and made an even **BIGGER** mess of the messy road.

A little while later, the town watched as Mater tried to drive on the new road. But the road was simply too **BUMPY**.

Doc was angry. He challenged Lightning to a race. "If you win, you go and I fix the road," said Doc. "If I win, you do the road **MY** way."

It certainly looked as if Lightning would win the race. But he didn't. He crashed into a cactus patch. Luckily, his new **friend**, Mater, helped him out.

After that, Lightning learned a few things.

He learned that the townsfolk were **proud** of their home.

He learned why Sally **loved** Radiator Springs.

And he learned that Doc had once been a *champion* race car.

Finally, Lightning fixed the road. Then he thanked all his new friends by getting spiffed up—Radiator Springs style!

Red the fire truck squirted Lightning **Clean**.

Guido and Luigi gave him new **tires**.

Ramone gave him a new **paint job**.

And Flo gave him a can of her **best oil**.

By that night, the townsfolk had fixed their shops and their **NEON** lights! The **OLD** town looked **NEW** again!

Soon it was time to go back to the racetrack. But now Lightning had Doc as his crew chief. He also had a new pit crew. And they weren't just his teammates— they were his new **best friends**.

Look Out for Mater!

Adapted by Andrea Posner-Sanchez
Illustrated by Ivan Boix Estudi

Times had changed in Radiator Springs. Once it was a sleepy little town. Now cars came from all over the world to visit the new racing headquarters of Lightning McQueen. The famous race car liked all the attention he got from his fans. But what he really enjoyed was spending time with his new friends.

Lightning's two closest friends were Mater and Sally.

Mater was a rusty tow truck with a silly sense of humor. He and Lightning McQueen were very different, but they had quickly become best buddies.

Sally was Lightning's "girlyfriend," as
Mater often said. She was caring and smart.
Lightning loved driving around with Sally
by his side.

One day, Sally and Lightning drove to a cliff overlooking a gravel pit. "That seems like a fun place to race," said Lightning. "I'll have to bring Mater there."

"Please don't," Sally begged. "I'm always warning Mater that this place is dangerous. I don't want to worry while I'm out of town the next few days. Promise me you'll look out for Mater while I'm away."

GRAVEL PIT

Back in town, Lightning was sadly rolling along Main Street when Mater came up beside him.

"Aw, shoot! Are you moping 'cause Miss Sally went away?" Mater asked his friend. "You need some Mater-style fu-un!"

Even though Lightning wasn't in the mood, he knew he'd better go along. After all, he had promised Sally he would look out for Mater.

Before long, Mater was speeding toward a grassy hill. "Slow down!" yelled Lightning. But Mater kept on going. The tow truck honked his horn and flew over the hill with a big grin.

Next, Mater drove down a winding dirt road—backward!

"You're crazy!" Lightning called to him. "Turn around!"

"Nah, it's more fun when you're looking the other way," Mater said, chuckling.

As the sun began to set, Mater insisted on going to one last place—the gravel pit!

"We can't go down there," Lightning said. "I promised Sally—"

GRAVEL PIT

Before the race car could even finish his sentence, Mater was revving his engine and speeding around the pit.

"Come on down!" cried Mater. "This is fu-un!"

KEEP OUT

Lightning realized that if he wanted to look out for Mater, he had better stay close to him. So the race car slowly inched his way down the slippery slope.

Mater rushed by, leaving Lightning behind in a cloud of dust.

Just then, the two friends heard a loud
"Ahem!" An angry bulldozer was coming up
behind them. "Stop messing up my gravel!"
he yelled. "This pit is not for playing in!"

Gulp! "Guess it's time to go!" cried
Lightning.

"Right behind ya, buddy," replied Mater.

The next day, Mater had a surprise for
his friend. Lightning followed Mater to . . .
the gravel pit.

"No way!" shouted Lightning. "Let's find
a safe place to have fun."

GRAVEL
PIT

"Shhh," whispered Mater as he rolled past the snoring bulldozer. "Big Bull's sleeping. And anyways, this time we won't even *touch* the gravel."

Before Lightning could stop him, Mater
rode onto some rails that had been set up to
help move gravel from one end of the pit to
the other. The race car watched as Mater
zoomed up and down the rails with a big smile
on his face. The tow truck honked
and hooted as he whooshed around
the turns.

Lightning knew he should stop Mater—
he had promised Sally. But it looked like such
fun! Lightning had to try, too.

Lightning made
his way to the top of
the track. He revved
his engine and took off.
"Ka-chow!" It was
fantastic!

"I told ya it was
fu-un!" Mater yelled.

"But Sally's right
about this place being
dangerous," said
Lightning. "Let's get
going before something
goes wrong."

But as the sun began to set, Mater insisted on one more ride. After a while, there was a loud *thwack!*

"You okay, buddy?" Lightning called into the darkness.

Suddenly, a floodlight lit the gravel pit. A booming voice shouted, "What is going on here?" Big Bull had woken up to find Mater hanging by his tow cable!

Luckily, Mater wasn't hurt. But he was stuck. "I can get you down," Big Bull fumed. "But I'll have to break your tow cable to do it."

Once Mater was free, he was as quiet as could be. What kind of tow truck was he without his cable?

Lightning felt bad, too. He should have done a better job looking out for Mater.

The next night, Sally came back to town. "Mater, what happened to you?" she gasped. When she found out that he and Lightning McQueen had been in the gravel pit, she was very angry.

"Lightning tried to warn me," said Mater. "I shoulda been a better friend and listened to him." He started to cry.

"You could have really been hurt," Sally said. "Thankfully, we can get that tow cable fixed."

Mater smiled and turned to his red friend. "Then we can go out for more Mater-style fu-un!"

Sally frowned. Lightning couldn't help laughing. "This time, I pick the place. I'll show you how to have Lightning McQueen–style fun—*without* getting hurt!"

Mater and the Ghost Light

Adapted by Andrea Posner-Sanchez

Illustrated by Bud Luckey and Dominique Louis

Mater liked to play pranks
on his friends.

Scary pranks were his favorites!

HEEYAA!

"Oh, buddy," Mater said to Lightning with a chuckle. "You looked like you just seen the Ghost Light!"

"What's that?" Lightning asked.

Sheriff came forward and told the story of the mysterious blue light that haunted Radiator Springs. "It all started on a night like tonight. A young couple were headed down this very stretch of the Mother Road when they spotted an unnatural blue glow . . . and before long, all that was left were two out-of-state license plates!"

"Don't be too scared, buddy. It ain't real," Mater whispered to Lightning.

"It *is* real!" shouted Sheriff. "And the one thing that angers the Ghost Light more than anything else . . . is the sound of clanking metal!"

When Sheriff finished his story, the townsfolk
said good night and quickly drove home.
Mater was left all alone—in the dark.

Gulp!

The scared tow truck drove to his shack in the junkyard. Mater thought he saw a monster in the shadows, but it was just a gnarled tree. He was trembling and shaking so much that his one good headlight fell off and broke.

Mater gasped as he saw a small glowing light
heading toward him.

"OH, NO!

It's the Ghost Light!"

The light flew right up to Mater's face. He opened one eye to peek at it.

"Oh, it's just a lightnin' bug," he said with a nervous laugh. "And anyhow, Sheriff said the Ghost Light is blue."

"The Ghost Light's right behind me!" Mater screamed.

"Now it's in front of me!" he gasped.

Mater raced through the tractor field.

He sped past Willys Butte.

But he couldn't get away from the Ghost Light.
"The Ghost Light's gonna eat me!" he cried.

A very tired Mater finally came to a stop and saw that the Ghost Light was just a lantern hanging from his tow cable. "Hey, wait a minute . . ."

"Gotcha!" Lightning said with a smile.

"Shoot," said Mater. "I knowed this was a joke the whole time."

"You see, son, the only thing to be scared of out here is your imagination," Sheriff told him.

"Yup. That and, of course, the *Screamin' Banshee*," added Doc.

"THE SCReamin' WHat?!?"